My Dad's the BEST!

NICHOLAS ALLAN

RED FOX

Some other books by Nicholas Allan:

Cinderella's Bum
Father Christmas Comes Up Trumps!
Father Christmas Needs a Wee!
Jesus' Christmas Party
Jesus' Day Off
Picasso's Trousers
The Prince and the Potty
The Royal Nappy
The Queen's Knickers
Where Willy Went

MY DAD'S THE BEST
A RED FOX BOOK 978 1 782 95530 6

Published in Great Britain by Red Fox,
an imprint of Random House Children's Publishers UK
A Penguin Random House Company

Penguin
Random House
UK

This edition published 2015

1 3 5 7 9 10 8 6 4 2

Red Fox Books are published by Random House Children's Publishers UK,
61–63 Uxbridge Road, London W5 5SA

www.randomhousechildrens.co.uk
www.randomhouse.co.uk

Addresses for companies within The Random House Group Limited can be found at: www.randomhouse.co.uk/offices.htm

THE RANDOM HOUSE GROUP Limited Reg. No. 954009

A CIP catalogue record for this book is available from the British Library.

Printed in China

Penguin Random House is committed to a sustainable future for our business, our readers and our planet.
This book is made from Forest Stewardship Council® certified paper.

MIX
Paper from
responsible sources
FSC
www.fsc.org FSC® C104723

Dad wears a suit of grey to work,
just like an elephant.

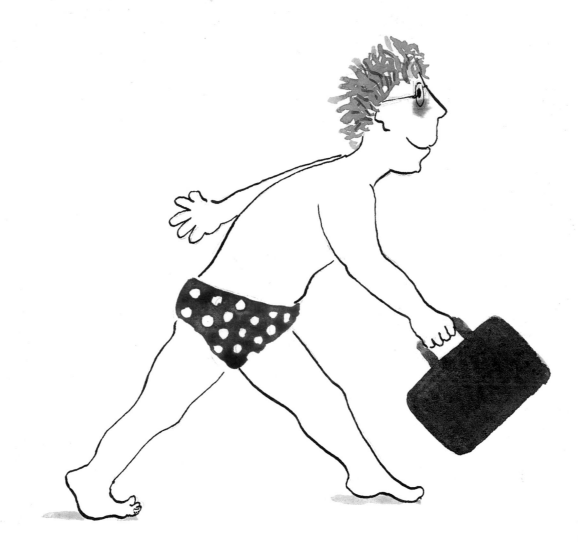

But underneath I know he wears
his blue and spotty **pants**.

He **helps** me with my homework,

in the evenings when he's there.

But **usually** when he's helping . . .

he is sleeping in his chair!

My dad is not the **strongest** dad.
Nor the strongest man alive . . .

And when he starts to **sing aloud**,
we all just run and hide.

It's just the same with dancing,
his arms and legs, they **flap**!

But he's like a ballet dancer . . .

when he gives me **piggybacks**!

My dad's a little **different**

but I **really** have to say

he may be **mad**, but I am **glad**,

he **always** makes my day.

My dad is not so **clever**
at maths and chemistry . . .

And my mum much prefers it
if he **does not** make our tea.

But in the fridge or cupboard, my dad will often see

a secret bar of **chocolate**, or a slice of cake for **me**.

My dad can never **master**

the simplest kind of tricks . . .

And can **never** put together
what I take to bits to fix.

But sometimes we just **make** things,
out of paper, glue and sticks . . .

Which is much more fun than fixing
what **any** dad can fix.

At weekends we go shopping . . .

Dad says, "Costs **too much** by far!"
But then we go to other shops . . .

and look at **BIG** new cars.

My dad simply **never** knows
where we're going when we walk.

And we don't **always** understand
what he's saying when he talks.

But **my** dad can tell me stories,
they come straight from his head . . .

And some of them are gory,
(he saves those ones for bed).

So then I find it hard to sleep.
They give me such a fright!

He tells me **more** and **more** of them,
and we stay awake all night!

My dad IS a little different.

He's **not** like all the rest.

He may be **mad**, but I am **glad** . . . .

MY dad's the VERY BEST!